P9-CLS-591

SALVAGE

The Ugly Duckling

HANS CHRISTIAN ANDERSEN

The Ugly Duckling

RETOLD AND ILLUSTRATED BY

TROY HOWELL

CRITTENBERGER LIBRARY
BLDG. 3271, 2ND DIV DR
FORT LEWIS, WA 98433-5000

G. P. Putnam's Sons
New York

COPY NO._____
PROPERTY OF U.S. ARMY
D-98-200

Text and illustrations copyright © 1990 by Troy Howell.
All rights reserved. This book, or parts thereof, may not be reproduced
in any form without permission in writing from the publisher.
G. P. Putnam's Sons, a division of The Putnam & Grosset Group,
200 Madison Avenue, New York, NY 10016. Published simultaneously in Canada.
Printed in Hong Kong by South China Printing Co. (1988) Ltd.
Book design by Golda Laurens.

Library of Congress Cataloging-in-Publication Data
Howell, Troy. Hans Christian Andersen's The ugly duckling/retold
and illustrated by Troy Howell. p. cm.
Summary: An ugly duckling spends an unhappy year ostracized by the
other animals before he grows into a beautiful swan.
{1. Fairy tales} I. Andersen, H. C. (Hans Christian), 1805–1875.
Grimme ælling. II. Title. III. Title: Ugly duckling.
PZ8.H84Han 1990 {E}—dc19 89-3781 CIP AC
ISBN 0-339-22158-1

1 3 5 7 9 10 8 6 4 2

First Impression

BOMC offers recordings and compact discs, cassettes
and records. For information and catalog write to
BOMR, Camp Hill, PA 17012.

For my sisters—
Teresa, Nancy, and Rebecca—
Good hearts are never proud.

Special thanks to Betty Schwartz

IT WAS SPLENDID in the country — it was summer! The wheatfields were golden, the oats were still green, and in the meadows the grass had been cut and put into stacks. An old stork stepped about on his long red legs chattering Egyptian, the language his mother had taught him. All around the fields and meadows were dense forests, and in the forests lay deep lakes. Indeed, it was splendid in the country.

In the midst of the sunshine stood a fine manor house, surrounded by a deep moat, and from its walls down to the water's edge grew great burdocks, so high that a child could stand under the loftiest leaves. It was as wild here as it was in the woods, and here a duck sat upon her nest, waiting for her eggs to hatch.

But it was such a long wait. She had grown tired and seldom had visitors. The other ducks preferred to swim in the moat than to sit and talk with her.

Finally one egg after another broke open. The yolks had come to life and were poking out their heads. "Peep! Peep!" the young ones cried.

"Quack! Quack! Quack!" called the mother, and the little ducklings scurried out, looking wide-eyed at the broad green leaves. The mother duck let them look as long as they liked, for green is good for the eyes.

"How big the world is!" they piped, for they had much more room now than when they were in their shells.

"Do you suppose this is all the world?" asked their mother. "Why, it reaches far beyond the garden, and into the parson's field, though I haven't been there yet. I hope you're all here."

She stood up.

"No, not all of you. The largest egg still remains. How long will this be? I'm really quite tired of it!"

She sat down again.

"Well, how goes it?" asked an old duck who had come by to call.

"It's so very long with this last one!" sighed the brooding duck. "It will not break. But just look at the others. Are they not the sweetest things you've ever seen? They're all like their father, the scamp! He never comes to see me."

"Let's have a look at the egg that won't hatch," the old duck said. "You can be sure it's a turkey's egg. I was cheated once in that way. There was no end to my worry and trouble, because turkeys are terrified of water. I could not get them to venture in!

I quacked and I clacked, but it was no use. Let me see the egg. Yes, it's a turkey's egg. Leave it alone, and teach your children to swim."

"I think I will sit a bit longer," replied the duck. "I've sat this long already."

"Do as you please," snapped the old duck, and away she waddled.

At last the great egg broke, too. "Peep! Peep!" cried the youngster, and crept forth. Oh—he was so big and ugly! Mother Duck scrutinized him.

"He's a frightfully large duckling," said she. "None of the others look like that. Could he really be a turkey's chick? Well, we shall soon find out. Into the water he must go, even if I have to push him in myself!"

The next day was beautiful, the sun shone brightly on the great burdock forest. The mother duck took her young ones to the water. Splash! In she sprang.

"Quack! Quack! Quack!" she called out, and one by one they all plunged in. The water closed over their heads, but the little ducklings popped up like corks and swam vigorously. Their legs knew just what to do. And the ugly gray duckling swam with them.

"Quack!" said the mother duck. "That's no turkey! How he uses his legs and carries himself! He's my very own! All in all, he can be handsome if you look at him right. Quack! Come along, and follow me into the wide, wide world and into the duckyard, where I'll introduce you. But stay close, so you won't be trodden on, and mind the cat!"

So they entered the duckyard. There was a mad scuffle going on. Two families were fighting over an eel's head, but the cat was the one who got it.

"See there, that is the way of the world!" Mother Duck said as she whetted her beak. She would have loved a taste of the eel's head herself. "Step smartly, now!" she admonished. "And bow down to the old duck yonder. She's the grandest of all here. She has Spanish blood, that's why she's so stout. Notice the red rag around her leg. That's a mark of distinction and the highest honor a duck can be paid. It means she's a favorite with her owner, and should be recognized by everyone. Look lively—don't turn in your toes! A cultured duck points out his toes, just as your father and mother do—like *so.* Now bow your heads politely and say 'Quack!'"

The ducklings did just that. But the other ducks looked round and groaned. "What! We don't want another lot of you! Aren't there enough of us already? And ugh! Look at that ugly thing! This is too much!" Whereupon one of the ducks flew over to the duckling and bit him on the neck.

"Leave him alone!" cried the mother. "He's done you no harm!"

"No, but he's too large and unsightly!" said the one who had nipped him. "He deserves a good smack!"

"Well, here's a pretty bunch," said the old duck with the rag around her leg. "They're all fair to look upon—except that one. How unfortunate. It's a pity you cannot remake him."

"Yes, I'm sorry it cannot be done, Your Grace," answered the mother. "He's not pretty to look at, but he has a good disposition, and swims as well as the others—better, I believe.

Maybe his looks will improve with age—and his size, as well. He was in the egg too long; that accounts for his misshapenness." She nudged his neck and smoothed his feathers. "Besides," she added, "looks aren't everything, for he's a drake, and strong. I'm sure he will make a place for himself."

"Well, your others are lovely enough," remarked the old duck. "Make yourselves at home, and if you should find an eel's head, bring it to me."

So they made themselves at home. But the poor duckling who had been the last to hatch, and who was such an eyesore, was bitten and abused by the ducks and hens alike. And the turkey-cock, who had been born with spurs and so thought he was an emperor, blew himself up like a full-rigged ship, and bore down upon the terrified duckling, crying, "Gobble, gobble, gobble!" until he was quite red in the face.

The tormented duckling knew neither where to sit nor where to stand, and was miserable over his own ugliness. He became the laughingstock of the duckyard.

That was the first day, and each day thereafter grew worse and worse. He was chased by everything in sight. His own brothers and sisters turned against him, saying, "If only the cat would get you, you loathsome wretch!"

Even his mother betrayed him. "Stay out of my sight!" she said.

"Shoo!" said the girl who fed the poultry, kicking at him.

Bitten and beaten, he ran away and flew over a fence. The birds in the bushes rose up in alarm. "That is because I'm so ugly," he thought, and closing his eyes, he kept on running. Eventually, he came to a vast moor, where the wild ducks lived. There he lay all the night, overcome by weariness.

At daybreak the ducks discovered him. "And of what sort are you?" they asked. The duckling turned round and round, bowing politely as best he knew how.

"You are quite ugly," they all exclaimed. "But that's no matter, as long as you don't marry into *our* family."

The duckling had no thoughts of marriage—far from it! He wanted only to swim among the reeds and sip the cool water.

Here he stayed the next two days, then two wild geese came—ganders they were, for they were males. They were still in their youth, which is why they were so bold.

"Listen, youngster," they said. "You're so lumpish that we like you. Why not come with us and be a bird of passage? Not far from here is another moor, with a lot of wild geese waiting, all unmarried, and able to cackle beautifully. You may make your fortune among them, ugly as you are."

"Boom! Boom!" Two shots rang out and both the ganders fell down dead. The water turned red with blood.

"Boom! Boom!" sounded two more shots, and the whole flock of geese flew up in a frenzy.

A great hunt was on. Hunters surrounded the swamp, and from every direction came the horrible sounds. Some huntsmen were even perched in the trees whose branches bent over the swamp. Blue smoke drifted through the leaves and over the water like fog. Hunting dogs came splashing by, crumpling the rushes on every side. It was a nightmare for the little duckling, who buried his head in his wing. Suddenly a monstrous dog appeared. His tongue rolled out, his glassy eyes shone, and he thrust out his nose and bared his teeth. Then—splash!—he went on, without harming the duckling.

"Oh, heaven be thanked!" he cried. "I am so ugly even a dog won't touch me!"

So he lay quite still as the blasts rang through the reeds and shot after shot was fired. Not until the late afternoon did the firing stop, and it was later still before the duckling dared to stir. Then he dashed away, out of the swamp. Over field and meadow he ran, and as he ran a fierce storm blew up, which he fought hard against.

Toward evening he came to a broken-down hut. It was in such a state of ruin that it couldn't decide which way to fall and so remained standing. The storm grew stronger and stronger, and the little duckling was forced to sit down to keep from being blown away. Then he saw that the door to the hut was off one hinge, creating a small crack. Through this he slipped.

An old woman lived in the hut with her cat and her hen. The cat, whose name was Sonny, could arch his back and purr, and give off sparks if you rubbed his fur the wrong way. The hen had short legs, and so was called Chickabiddy Shortshanks. She was a good layer, and the woman loved her as if she were her very own child.

In the morning they noticed the strange duckling. The hen clucked and the cat purred.

"What is this?" asked the woman, looking here and there, for her eyesight was bad. She thought a fat duck had strayed in. "What good fortune!" she said. "Now there'll be duck eggs—if it is not a drake. We shall soon see."

So the duckling was taken on trial for three weeks—but no eggs came.

Now the cat was the master of the house, and the hen was the mistress. They always declared: "We and the world," for they

thought of themselves as half of the world, and the better half at that. The duckling thought he might offer a different opinion, but the hen would not have it.

"Can you lay eggs?" she asked.

"No."

"Then keep silence whilst wisdom is speaking."

The duckling withdrew to a corner, ill-humored. Then he remembered the fresh air and the sunshine, and felt such a longing to be on the water he had to tell the hen of it.

"What has crept into your head?" the hen said. "You're idle, that's why you imagine things! Lay an egg or two, or take up purring, and it will pass."

"But it is so delightful on the water!" said the duckling. "So wonderful to dip underneath and dive to the bottom!"

"Yes, I'm sure it's just marvelous!" the hen croaked. "I believe you've lost your mind! Ask the cat, he's the cleverest one I know. See what *he* thinks of your dipping and diving! I won't say what *I* think. Or ask the old woman, no one on earth is smarter than she. Do you think she wishes to swim and bury her head in the water? Be sensible."

"But you don't understand," cried the duckling. "I think I will go out into the wide world."

"Then, you just *do* that!" said the hen.

And so the duckling left. He swam, he dived, but he was still shunned by all who met him.

UTUMN CAME. The leaves turned yellow, then brown; they danced in the wind as they fell. The air grew chill, the clouds hung low, heavy with snow and hail. On a fence a raven cried, "C-c-caw!" he was so cold. It would make one shiver to think of it. How miserable the duckling must have been!

One evening, as the sun was setting, a great flock of handsome birds rose up from the trees. They were dazzlingly white, with long willowy necks. They were swans. Their cries were strange as they spread their glorious wings and soared away to warmer, faraway lands and lakes. They mounted up high, so high! As he watched, a peculiar feeling came over the little duckling. He spun round and round in the water, craned his neck toward them, and cried out so piercingly that he frightened himself.

The image of those stately birds would never leave his memory, and when they had gone he dove down deep and came up again, quite beside himself. He did not know their name nor whither they went, yet his heart was drawn to them like nothing before. He was not envious of them, the wish for such loveliness was beyond all his thoughts. He would have been glad to have been received by the ducks alone—the poor creature!

WINTER BECAME COLD, bitter cold! The duckling had to swim steadily about in the water to keep it from freezing. But every night the space in which he swam became smaller and smaller. The ice all around him crackled and groaned. He was compelled to move his legs continually to stop it from closing in. But at last he lay still, quite exhausted, and thus froze fast into the ice.

Early the next morning a farmer passed by and saw what had happened. With his wooden shoe he broke the ice, and carried the duckling home to his wife. There the duckling revived. The children wanted to play with him, but he thought they meant to do him harm, so in his fright he flew into the milk pan, spattering milk across the room. The woman screamed and threw up her hands, which sent the poor bird into the butter tub and then into the meal barrel and out again. What a sight he was! The woman shrieked and swung at him with the fire tongs. The children laughed and screeched and tumbled over each other trying to catch him. It was well the door stood open, for through it he escaped and ran past the brambles and into the newly fallen snow. There he lay dazed.

It is too sad to tell all the sufferings he had to endure that long winter.

SPRING CAME AT LAST.

The sun was shining warmly again and the larks began to sing. The world was waking up and blossoming. And the duckling was there on the moor among the rushes. He was much stronger and older now. All at once he lifted his wings to fly. They beat the air and bore him up!

Before he knew it he had arrived in a grand garden, where the elder trees smelled sweet and bent down their long branches to the winding canals. It was beautiful here. And look! There were three glorious swans coming out of the thicket. They rustled their great wings and glided across the water. The duckling recognized them and felt a strange melancholy.

"I will fly to them, those royal birds!" he said. "And they will beat me because I, who am so ugly, dare to be with them. But so be it. I would rather be killed by *them* than be bitten by the ducks, pecked at by the hens, and suffer through another hard winter."

He flew to them, alighting on the water.

The swans started toward him with outstretched wings.

"Kill me!" he cried, and lowered his head, ready for death.

But what did he see in the water below him? He saw there his own image, no longer a clumsy, ugly gray thing, hated and despised. He himself was a swan!

No matter if one has been born in the duckyard, so long as one comes from a real swan's egg!

CRITTENBERGER LIBRARY
BLDG. 3271, 2ND DIV DR
FORT LEWIS, WA 98433-5000

Now he was glad to have endured so much sorrow and hardship—the greater was the splendor and joy before him. The swans encircled him and stroked him with their beaks. He was accepted as one of their own.

Little children came running into the garden with bread and grain to offer.

"Look!" called the youngest. "A new one has come!"

They clapped and they danced, and ran to their parents, who brought more bread and cake to cast on the water.

"This new one is more beautiful than them all," they said. "So young and handsome!"

And the other swans bowed their heads to him.

Then he felt quite ashamed, and hid his head under his wing, not knowing what to do. He was very happy, but very humbled, for a good heart is never proud.

He thought of how he had been mistreated and mocked, and now was praised for his beauty. Even the elder trees bent low their branches for him, and the sun shone down splendidly.

He ruffled his feathers and raised his slender neck, and sang out with a full heart: "I never dreamed of so much happiness when I was the ugly duckling!"

*The illustrations for this book were
rendered in acrylic paints with oil glazing.
The text was set in Garamond no. 3.*